For Mr. Schu, who's never horrible.
—A.D.

For Lydia, O Bear, and Chomper.
—Z.O.

SNAP!

HORRIBLE
BEAR!

Written by **Ame Dyckman**   Illustrated by **Zachariah OHora**

L B

Little, Brown and Company
New York Boston

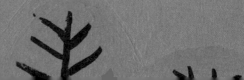

A girl peeked into Bear's cave.

She reached—
but he rolled.

CRUNCH!

HORRIBLE
BEAR!

the girl shouted.

She stomped all the way home.

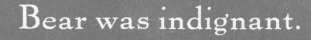

Bear was indignant.

"I'M not horrible!" he said.

"SHE barged in!"

"SHE made a ruckus.

"SHE woke ME up!" "How would SHE like it if—"

Bear got an idea.

It was a Horrible Bear idea.

Bear practiced barging.

He practiced making a ruckus.

He practiced waking
someone up.

HORRIBLE BEAR!

Bat squeaked.

"Perfect!"
Bear said.

Bear stomped out of his cave.

The girl stomped into her room.

But she was too upset to nap.
So, the girl tried drawing.

She tried reading.

She tried talking to the best listener she knew.

THAT HORRIBLE BEAR!

"He broke my—"

RIP!

Suddenly, her stuffie couldn't listen as well as before.

"I didn't mean to!" the girl cried.

"Oh."

He stomped through the meadow.

He stomped straight to the girl's front door—

which opened.

I'M SORRY!

the girl said.

And all the horrible went right out of Bear.

Bear patted.

He wiped.

He got another idea.

It was a Sweet Bear idea.

"Thank you, Bear,"
the girl whispered.

She had a
Sweet Bear idea,
too.

Bear and the girl skipped through the meadow.

They bounced up the mountain.

And together, they patched everything up.

Even the kite.

Nothing was horrible at all . . .

AUTHOR'S NOTE

I lost a kite once. The string snapped, and my new kite
sailed away—maybe into a bear's cave. I hope the bear liked it.
—*Ame Dyckman*

ARTIST'S NOTE

The art for *Horrible Bear!* was created using acrylic paint on
90-pound acid-free Stonehenge printing paper. The story inspired me
to buy lots of kites and overcome my fear of using the color purple.
—*Zachariah OHora*

ABOUT THIS BOOK

This book was edited by Bethany Strout and designed by Saho Fujii. The production
was supervised by Erika Schwartz, and the production editor was Barbara Bakowski.
This book was printed on 140 gsm Gold Sun woodfree. The text was set in LTC Pabst
Oldstyle, and the display type was hand-lettered.

PRINTED IN CHINA